DIARY OF YOYO JR.

Big Brother

Written and illustrated by
Tanya Koles

Diary of YoYo Jr.
Big Brother

This book is based on the characters of the YouTube channels

Monkey Baby YoYo and *Family YoYo*.

The photo illustrations created from the videos

are used with the permission of the

channel owner and creator Nguyen Van Ky.

First Edition: February 2022

Self-Match Press

Texas, USA

To my friend

_____

KEEP READING EVERY DAY!

YoYo Jr.

When I first heard that I'd have a little sister,
I decided to get ready.
Well, honestly, this is not how it happened.
First, I didn't even know what a sister was.
My Dad explained that a sister was
a little girl, and that Mom would
bring her from the hospital.

"Could you take care of this doll?" he asked.
"I want to make sure I can trust you with Ai Tran."
"Who is Ai Tran?" I asked. Then it dawned
on me, "She is my little sister!"

I did the best I could. Even when
I had to eat or drink,
I would not let go of the doll.

I missed my Mom a lot. So, Dad took me to visit her in the hospital.

"Where is Ai Tran?" I kept on asking.
"She hasn't arrived yet," my Mom said.
"Is she coming soon?"
"Very soon. Be patient, YoYo."

I didn't mind. I could be patient. In fact, I wasn't even sure
if I wanted to see Ai Tran that much.
What if Mom and Dad liked her more than me?
What if they spent all their time with her and I would be left alone?

I was scared. I wanted to be a little baby again,
not a big brother. As if sensing my fear, Mom gave me
a milk bottle. I snuggled in her arms feeling safe and peaceful.
"I'll worry about Ai Tran when she arrives," I thought.

Mom and Ai Tran finally came home. My sister was not what I'd expected. I've seen girls before. They could run and jump and made great playmates. This one didn't even move. I was disappointed. I was more interested in my Mom's hand than in Ai Tran. Or, maybe I was a little jealous because Mom kept on touching and patting her.

At last, the pink bundle moved and made some noise.
"All right, maybe I'll give her a chance," I thought at that
moment.

I didn't know that being a big brother meant
so much extra work.
I often had to get something for Ai Tran, for example,
bring her a diaper, fetch a box with wipes, or hand a can with
baby formula.

Ai Tran was so helpless. She couldn't do anything for herself.
I felt sorry for Ai Tran so I tried to help
as much as I could.

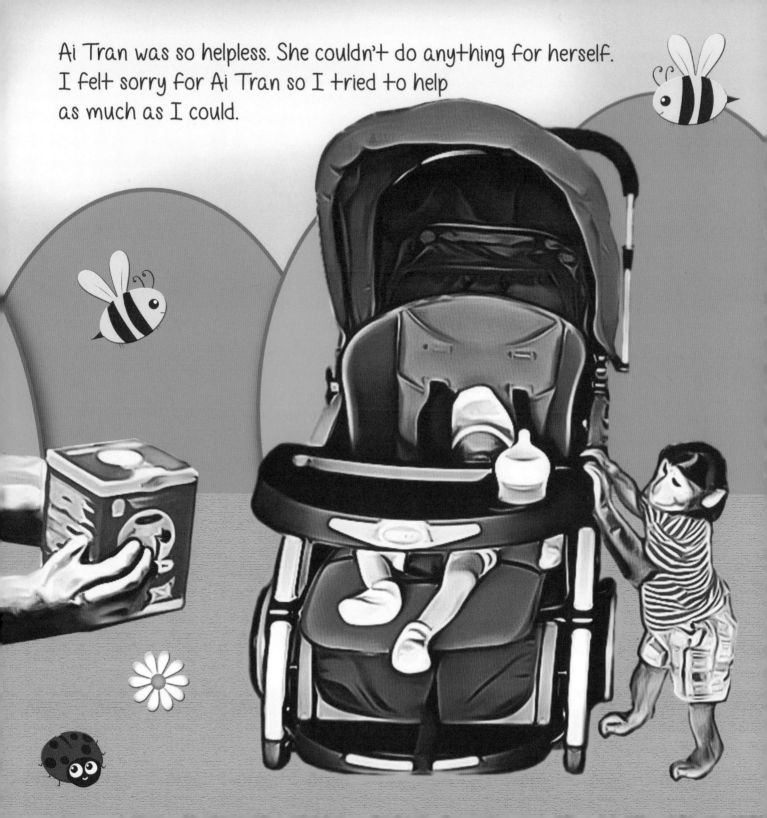

It wasn't always easy to get along with Ai Tran. She was no angel. She would grab and pull my shirt very hard for no reason. I didn't like it but I always remained calm.

As time passed, Ai Tran learned to do new things.
She was more fun to be with.
Sometimes we pretended that we
were swimming in the ocean.

And sometimes, we swam
for real, but it was usually
in the bathtub.

I am a great swimmer, by the way.
I can even swim underwater
with my eyes open.

STRANGER DANGER!

Once a stranger got into our house.
He wanted to take away Ai Tran.
I was ready to protect her.
I found a big stick and made
it very clear:

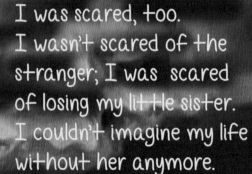

If you don't get out, I'll hit you

The stranger left.
He got scared of me.
Only then I realized that
I was scared, too.
I wasn't scared of the
stranger; I was scared
of losing my little sister.
I couldn't imagine my life
without her anymore.

I would like to say that Ai Tran and I started to have
the best relationship ever. That wouldn't be true.
Ai Tran had this awful habit of taking things away from me.
When my Dad finally allowed me to play with his iPhone,
Ai Tran reached out and grabbed it with her two little hands.

I got upset and tried to get the phone back. Ai Tran started crying. I don't like when my sister cries, but I kept on pulling. My Dad noticed we were not getting along. He borrowed my Mom's iPhone and gave it to Ai Tran. She immediately stuck it in her mouth. I couldn't stand how she handled technology, so I looked away and enjoyed my time with my phone.

It happens a lot with toys. Ai Tran loves my toys, and I love them, too. I don't always want to share my toys with her. My Mom and Dad tell me to share. I usually don't mind, but not when it comes to my favorite rubber fish. That one is off limits. Does that make me a bad big brother?

In my defense, when someone else takes toys from
Ai Tran, I always come to the rescue.
I like my cousin Tin, but I don't let
 him play with Ai Tran's toys.
They belong to her.

One day Ai Tran got sick.
I touched her right ear,
and it was hot.

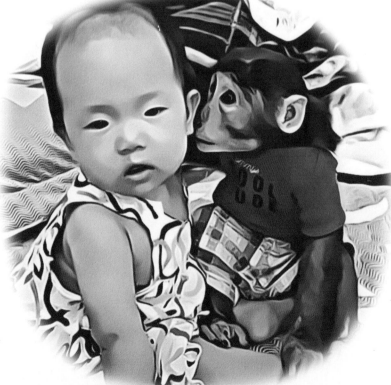

I touched her left ear;
it was burning hot.

I went and got a thermometer
to make sure I was not
imagining things.
Ai Tran had a fever of 102 degrees.

I had to do something.
I opened the fridge and
took out an ice patch.
"This will help her to cool
down", I thought.

Ai Tran didn't like the ice patch on her forehead. She started crying. I tried to help her calm down by placing a wet cloth on her head.

I didn't leave Ai Tran's side until her fever broke down.
After a couple of hours, she started feeling better.
I was relieved. Again, I realized that I could only be happy
knowing that my sister was all right.

Ai Tran continued to grow. She soon learned how to crawl. I was so excited to see her move from place to place. She was turning into a sister I've always wanted.

She took her first steps with the help of a blue duck-faced walker. I didn't care. My sister could now walk! I could chase after her, and she could chase after me.

For some reason, Ai Tran didn't like the fancy blue walker that much.
She preferred the old wooden red walker instead.
We would play with it first, and then Ai Tran would take it for a spin.

She would require a lot of help from me and my dad. I would show her many times how to do it right, but she would still struggle to stay straight and keep her balance.

I couldn't understand why walking was so difficult for Ai Tran.

I was proud of my little sister. She never gave up, and soon she was walking on her own.

Now with Ai Tran able to crawl and walk, we became the best playmates ever. Finally, my dream of having fun with my little sister came true.

I am very happy to have
my loving family, and especially,
my dear sister Ai Tran.
Bye-bye! Thank you for reading my diary.

Watch YoYo Jr. on

https://www.youtube.com/c/MonkeyYoYoFunny

https://www.youtube.com/c/monkeyBabyYoYoCute

Another Title Available

Printed in Great Britain
by Amazon

34316656R00021